For Owen & Elly,
It all began with you.
Love, Mama (Ashley)

Different Roads
Your ASD authority since 1995

Copyright: Ashley Abeles

Illustrated and designed by: Melissa DiPeri Design, LLC.

Different Roads to Learning, Inc.
121 West 27th Street, Suite 1003B
New York, New York 10001

Telephone: 800 853 1057
Fax: 800 317 0146

www.difflearn.com or info@difflearn.com

Printed in China

ISBN: 978-0-9910403-2-2

LCCN: 2018958014

KINDNESS
DETECTIVE

written by: Ashley Abeles, MSEd

illustrated by: Melissa DiPeri

On one sunny Monday, Owen arose
And got dressed in his sunny school clothes.
He brushed his tooth and hopped on his bus,
Happy to see his good friend, Russ.

Later that day, when they went to recess,
Owen noticed that Russ looked distressed.
Owen wondered why Russ might feel sad
When this was a place *he* always felt glad!

1

Owen decided to step into his shoes
To see things from a new point of view.
And when he did, he could see

things a little differently.

Each day at recess, his classmates played games
And chose different teams by calling out names.
Often the teams had chosen Russ last
Because some children felt he was not fast.

LAVERNE

RAUL

OWEN

RENEE

Once Owen saw things from Russ's perspective,
He turned himself into a Kindness Detective.

How could he help? What could he do?
What would you do if Owen were YOU?

Owen now realized that Russ felt left out
And *this* he was able to do something about.
When it was his turn, he called Russ's name.
Russ was no longer the last in the game!

On one windy Tuesday, Owen arose
And got dressed in his windy school clothes.
He ate his breakfast and rode to school,
Excited to meet his new classmate, Raul.

Raul walked in and Owen said, "Hey!"
But Raul dropped his head and turned away.
Owen wondered why Raul didn't look,
Play with toys, or read a book.

Owen decided to step into his shoes
To see things from a new point of view.
And when he did, he could see

things a little differently.

Raul had just moved and this school was brand-new.
He had left his old home and all his friends, too.
He wanted new friends but was feeling shy.
Raul looked away so he would not cry.

Classroom Rules
1. Listening Bodies.
   I will listen and follow directions.
2. Raised Hands
   I will raise my hand to share ideas.
3. Quiet Mouths
   I will use a soft voice.
4. Walking Feet
   I will walk in school and be safe.
5. Helping Hands
   I will use hands for helping and not hurting.

Once Owen saw things from Raul's perspective,
He turned himself into a Kindness Detective.

How could he help? What could he do?
What would you do if Owen were YOU?

Owen now saw that Raul just felt scared
And might need to know that somebody cared.
Owen, too, had switched neighborhoods
And let Raul know that he understood.

On one rainy Wednesday, Owen arose
And got dressed in his rainy school clothes.
He combed his hair and got ready to learn,
Along with his next-door neighbor, Laverne.

During lunch, Owen offered a snack,
But Laverne used a napkin to push it right back.
Owen felt hurt; he was trying to share.
Why did his friend seem not to care?

Owen decided to step into her shoes
To see things from a new point of view.
And when he did, he could see

things a little differently.

Laverne was not rude or feeling ungrateful.
She has food allergies and needs to be careful.
She wanted a snack and loved that he cared,
But that was not food she was able to share.

Once Owen saw things from Laverne's perspective,
He turned himself into a Kindness Detective.
How could he help? What could he do?
What would you do if Owen were YOU?

Owen now realized that when they had treats,
They often were foods that Laverne could not eat.
They talked to their teacher and made a new rule
That class snacks must be safe for all students at school.

12

On one cloudy Thursday, Owen arose
And got dressed in his cloudy school clothe
He washed his face and hugged his mom,
Then rushed to school to see Elam.

During math, Elam put his head down.
He covered his eyes and started to frown.
Owen loved math and just couldn't see
Why his friend would feel so unhappy.

Owen decided to step into his shoes
To see things from a new point of view.
And when he did, he could see

things a little differently.

Elam was creative, smart, and amusing.
He just found math class a little confusing.
Elam tried his best, but it was still tough,
And that Thursday morning he just had enough.

Once Owen saw things from Elam's perspective
He turned himself into a Kindness Detective.

How could he help? What could he do?
What would you do if Owen were YOU?

Though Owen loved math and thought it was fun,
This was not true for everyone.
So, Owen leaned over and offered some guidance
And later, Elam helped Owen in science.

On one snowy Friday, Owen arose
And got dressed in his snowy school clothes.
He packed his bag and prepared for the day,
Then went to his classroom to see Renee.

When they turned in their homework, Renee had non
Owen wondered, *why wasn't it done?*
Homework was due every day.
Didn't she know it worked this way?

Owen decided to step into her shoes
To see things from a new point of view.
And when he did, he could see

things a little differently.

Renee always studied with great results,
But this week, things at home had been difficult.
Her mom had been sick, and her dog ran away,
So, she could not do her homework that day.

Once Owen saw things from Renee's perspective,
He turned himself into a Kindness Detective.

How could he help? What could he do?
What would you do if Owen were YOU?

19

Owen decided that after school,
He would look for Renee's puppy, too.
Along with their parents, they searched all around,
And no one gave up until he was found.

20

On Saturday morning, Owen arose
And got dressed in his soccer clothes.
With Raul and Elam, he started to play,
As they waited for Russ, Laverne, and Renee.

Together, they kicked the ball around,
But suddenly Owen looked to the ground.
He walked off the field with a frustrated face.
His friends wondered what had just taken place.

They decided to step into his shoes
To see things from a new point of view.
And when they did, they could see

things a little differently.

Owen practiced every day
But struggled to put a goal away.
He really wanted to help his team score.
He truly wanted to help his team more.

Once his friends saw things from Owen's perspective,
They turned themselves into Kindness Detectives.

How could they help? What could they do?
What would you do if they were YOU?

They assured Owen that it was okay -
All of them missed some shots that day.
Whether they lost or whether they won,
The best part of soccer was having fun!

On one Sunday morning, Owen arose
And did not dress in dressy clothes.
In his pajamas, he reflected
On how he and his friends were **connected**.

25

They all faced troubles others had not known,
And all of them sometimes felt alone.
But when they walked in each other's shoes,
They could see each other's views.
So...

ELAM

RENEE

RUSS

When you need a little perspective,
Turn yourself into a Kindness Detective.
And when you do, you might discover
We are all very much like each other.

LAVERNE

OWEN

RAUL

We may have different backgrounds or names,
Troubles, talents, or favorite games,
But all of us sometimes need a friend,
And all of us have some kindness to lend.